When it comes to Billy the Kid, I could call it puppy love (the title of my very first record). I've loved Billy since he was a tiny little pup with big ears. Now he's full-grown—still with big ears! I loved him then, I love him now, and will always do so. He is my god-dog. I love those sayings that "Dog is God spelled backwards" and "A dog is man or woman's best friend." We have a lot in common, Billy the Kid and I. We both know what it feels like to be bullied—me in my real-life childhood, and he in the story of *Billy the Kid Makes It Big*. I used the theme to one of my songs called "Makin' Fun Ain't Funny," because I think it has a great message and made for a good little story—or at least I hope you think so.

I could write about Billy the Kid from now on and probably will, as there are so many stories to tell. Stay tuned, and enjoy the first book of the many adventures of Billy the Kid.

Love,

*Dolly*

Dolly Pawton
Whoops!
Parton

# DOLLY PARTON'S
## BILLY THE KID MAKES IT BIG

## Text by Dolly Parton
with Erica S. Perl
Lyrics by Dolly Parton
Art by MacKenzie Haley

Penguin Workshop

**Billy the Kid** was born with an ear for music.

Music made Billy feel connected to something bigger than himself.

At the pluck of a guitar string, he'd race over and bark to the beat.

Whenever he closed his eyes, he dreamed of having his own country band so he could make great music with great friends.

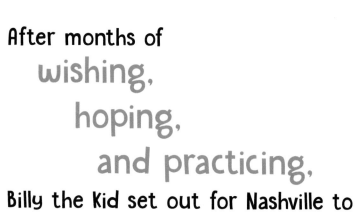

After months of
wishing,
hoping,
and practicing,
Billy the Kid set out for Nashville to make his dream come true.

As soon as he arrived, he explored downtown, sniffing out the city sights.

When a sign caught his eye, his stubby tail began to wag.
This is it!

Quickly, Billy joined the sign-up line.
"New around here?" asked a large dog.

Billy nodded. "How'd you know?"

"Lucky guess." The dog grinned. "Name's Big Earl. This here's my band."

"Nice to meet you," said Billy. "Maybe we could jam sometime?"

"You? Play with us?" Big Earl laughed. "You're barking up the wrong tree."

"You're clearly not a true muttropolitan like us," added Big Pearl, her nose in the air.

"Beat it, kid," bellowed Big Merle.

Billy the Kid tucked his tail between his legs and ran.

WHAT WAS I THINKING, COMING TO NASHVILLE? THOSE DOGS ARE RIGHT. I DON'T BELONG HERE.

Billy felt lower than a stick on the ground. He ate some flowers. That helped a little.

Then, he strummed his guitar.
That helped a lot.

And I will pawlways love you ♪♫♪

Jowlene Jowlene Jowlene

It had been a ruff day.
Music always made him feel better.

The sound of applause took Billy by surprise.
"You're pawsitively perfect," said Bo.
"Yeah!" agreed Binky. "Wanna join our band?"
"Y'all don't want me," Billy told them. "I'm not big-city material."

Bo made a face. "You clearly love making music. That's what we're about."

Billy wasn't sure what to say until Buster, the tiniest pup, finally broke the silence.

When Billy nodded, the little dogs cheered.
"To the studio!" said Bo. "The Battle of the Bow-Wows is tomorrow!"

It was a long night.
But by sunup, Billy the Kid had to admit: *We don't sound half bad.*

On the way to the Battle, though,
Billy began to get nervous.

It got worse backstage when Billy heard a familiar voice.

"Who let you in, pip-squeak?" asked Big Earl.

"And *what* are you wearing?" added Big Pearl.

Billy froze.

And then he realized they weren't talking to him.
"They're picking on Buster!" cried Binky.
Bo gasped. "What do we do?"

Billy's hackles rose.
He wished someone would teach those big dogs a lesson.
Then he realized who could.
"Follow me," he growled.

A few minutes later, a huge shadow fell across
Earl, Pearl, and Merle.
   It was the biggest dog they'd ever seen.
   "Who gave you the right to bully Buster?"
boomed the Biggest Dog.
   "Relax," said Big Earl. "We were just havin' fun."

"You weren't havin' fun. You were makin' fun," the Biggest Dog said,

"AND MAKIN' FUN AIN'T FUNNY."

Earl, Pearl, and Merle didn't stick around
to hear any more.
They howled and headed for the hills.

# "PAW RIGHT!"

The pups shed their disguise.
"Thanks, y'all," said Buster.
Billy and his bandmates embraced.

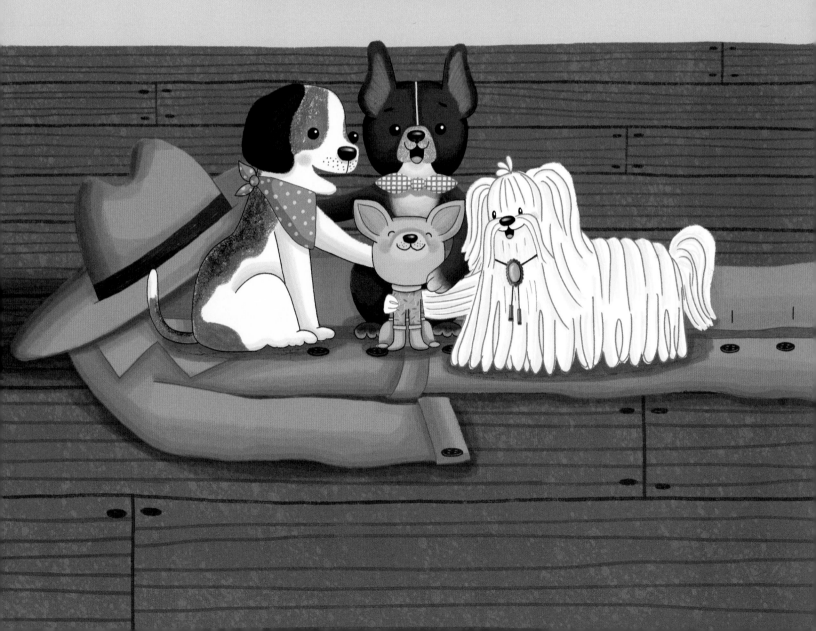

# Battle of the Bow-Wows

The lights dimmed.
The Battle of the Bow-Wows began.
It was an epic Battle.

Dogs crooned.

Dogs twanged.

Dogs howled, and
wailed, and sang.

When it was Billy's turn to perform, his heart was beating double-time.
But soon he began to relax and enjoy himself.
He finally felt like he was right where he belonged.

At the awards ceremony, Billy's band got a standing ovation.
It was totally pawsome!

Afterward, they took a walk and ended up at a magnificent music hall.

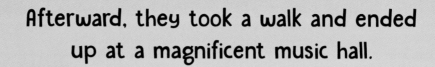

"This has been a night I'll always remember," said Billy the Kid.

BEST
NEW
ACT

"Me too," said Bo. "We rocked, and our trophy is huge!"

Just then, Billy's favorite singer stepped onstage.
Her warm voice reminded him why he came to Nashville.

"The trophy's great," Billy said to his friends,
"but I feel like we won something even bigger."

To Franny Sewell, whose amazing voice, heart, and mind will take her far—ESP

For Cousin Jen. Finally, a whole book about dogs, not cats—MH

PENGUIN WORKSHOP
An imprint of Penguin Random House LLC, New York

First published in the United States of America by Penguin Workshop,
an imprint of Penguin Random House LLC, New York, 2023

Text copyright © 2023 by Dolly Parton
Lyrics copyright © 2017 by Dolly Parton
Illustrations copyright © 2023 by Penguin Random House LLC

Visit us online at penguinrandomhouse.com.

Library of Congress Control Number: 2023930688

Printed in the United States of America

ISBN 9780593661574          10 9 8 7 6 5 4 3 2 1 WOR

Design by Lynn Portnoff

# MAKIN' FUN AIN'T FUNNY

## BY DOLLY PARTON

Don't do it, don't do it,
Makin' fun ain't funny.
Don't do it, don't do it,
Makin' fun ain't funny.

Don't do this, makin' someone else feel small
To make yourself look big.
If you can't be big, don't belittle someone else.
That's not the thing to do.

Don't do it, don't do it,
Makin' fun ain't funny.
Don't do it, don't do it,
Makin' fun ain't funny.

It's not cool to be a bully
Actin' ugly, breakin' all the rules.
Don't do that.
How would you feel if you'z the one that they were laughin' at?
How would you feel?

Don't do it, don't do it,
Makin' fun ain't funny.
Don't do it, don't do it,
Makin' fun ain't funny.

It hurts, and it hurts worse when it is done by so-called friends.
I promise you that it will come to no good in the end.
Bullies never ever get respect from anyone.
Let's celebrate our differences instead of making fun.

Just don't do it, don't do it,
Makin' fun ain't funny.
Don't do it, don't do it,
Not on a dare, for show or money.

Don't do it, don't do it,
Makin' fun ain't funny.
Don't do it, don't do it,
Makin' fun ain't funny.

Don't do it, don't do it,
Makin' fun ain't funny.
Don't do it, don't do it,
Makin' fun ain't funny.

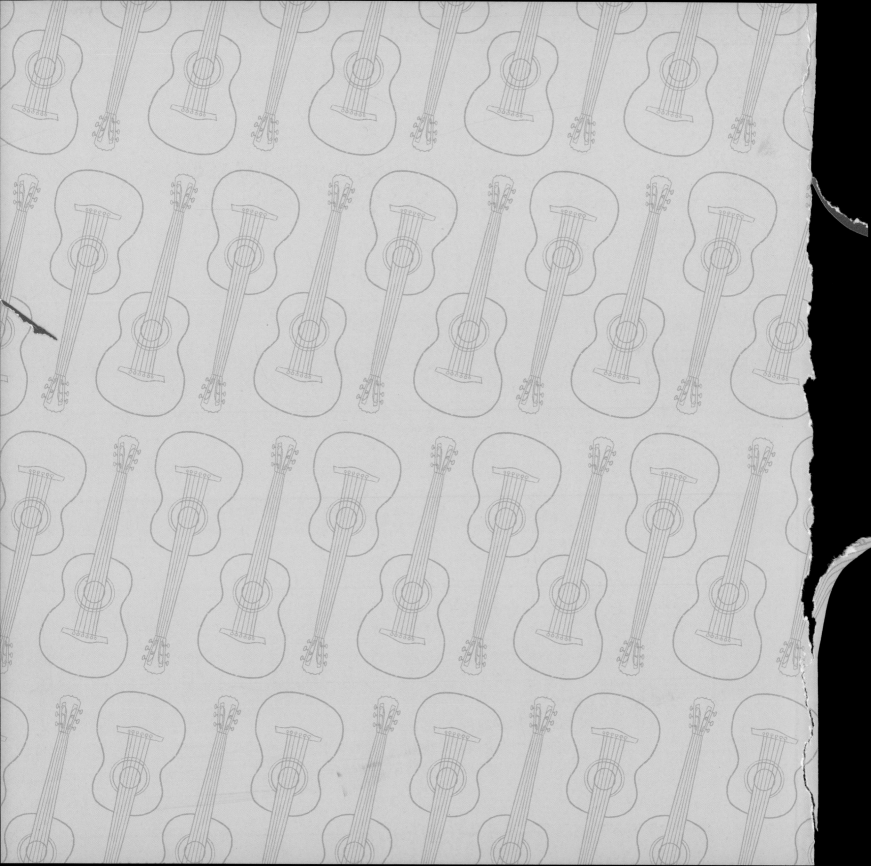